English text Alison Winn

HODDER AND STOUGHTON
LONDON SYDNEY AUCKLAND TORONTO

Gunilla Wolde

Different Peter and Emma

This is Emma.

This is Emma too.
But now she looks different because her hair is done up in bunches and tied with two bows.

This is Peter.

Peter and Emma are the same age.
But they look quite different from each other.

Sometimes Emma goes home with Peter.
Peter's house is very different from Emma's house.
It is quite small and only *his* family live in it.
Emma lives in a very *big* house where lots of
families live in flats.

Peter thinks *that*
must be *very* different.

In Emma's family there is a Mummy and a Daddy. They take it in turns to stay at home and look after Emma and baby brother.
At Peter's house it is different.

There is no Daddy.
Instead there is a nice kind
Grannie who is at home all the time
with Peter and his dog.
Peter's mother is at work
all day long.

Emma gets quite used to having baby brother around all the time. Sometimes she gets tired of playing with him.

Peter thinks it must be nice and
different having a baby around.
He really *likes* playing with
Emma's baby brother.

Peter thinks there is nothing very special
about having a dog.
Sometimes he wishes his dog would stop
being such a nuisance.

Emma thinks how nice and different it would be to have a dog instead of a baby. She could romp and roll around all day with a dog. If only she had one.

When Emma plays alone all her games seem the same. She knows exactly what she is going to do next – and nothing is ever different.

But when Peter plays with Emma, well that's _quite_ different. Peter and Emma can think up the most exciting games to play together.

Sometimes they dress up in funny old clothes and try to look alike.

But they usually end up looking rather different.

Bother – the light has gone out.
It seems very different in the dark.
Emma can't see Peter, and Peter can't see Emma.

But soon their eyes get used to the gloom.
Now they can see just a little. They wriggle
and giggle and try to catch each other.

When the light goes on everything seems different and ordinary.
Emma wants to look like Emma again.
And Peter wants to look like Peter.
And they *both* want their elevenses.

Now the sandwiches taste different.
Some taste of potted meat,
and some taste of cheese.

Well, it seems as if there is something
different about almost everything.
That's good.
If everything was always alike *all* the time,
how very dull it would be.